Things You'll Learn If You Live Long Enough So You Might As Well Know Now

_____

NAME

_____

FROM

_____

DATE

ISBN: 0-931089-81-6

A Special Message:

_____

_____

_____

_____

_____

_____

_____

_____

_____

_____

_____

_____

_____

_____

—— **66** ——

If you are going to stand on thin ice, you might as well dance.

—— **99** ——

——————— 66 ———————

Going to college
won't guarantee
you a job, but it'll
give you four
years to worry
about getting one.

——————— 99 ———————

——— **66** ———

Never go to a doctor whose office plants have died.

——— **99** ———

"

Our dads really hated it when we said, 'My dad can whip your dad'!

"

—— 66 ——

If Benjamin Franklin had tried to be a general and George Washington had tried to be an inventor, we would probably be living in a British colony without electricity.

—— 99 ——

Chivalry
isn't dead.

It's just resting.

"

Being right doesn't count until the right people know you're right.

"

———— 66 ————

Committee
work is like a
soft chair — easy
to get into, but
hard to get
out of.

———— 99 ————

"

There are two
ways to handle
a woman, and
nobody knows
either of them.

"

"

Be kind to your parents. After sending you through college, you're all they have left.

"

—— 66 ——

If people listened to themselves more often, they would talk less.

—— 99 ——

66

Money won't buy
happiness, but it
will pay the salaries
of a large research
staff to study the
problem.

99

"

'*I tried, but it didn't work*' is a lot better than '*I wish I'd tried.*'

"

66

Management is the art of getting other people to do all the work.

99

———— " ————

Women will wear anything ludicrous-looking if it's "in style"...

———— " ————

"

... Men don't know *what* they've got on.

"

———— " ————

God gave you
two ears and
one mouth . . . so
you should listen
twice as much
as you talk.

———— " ————

— 66 —

The person who knows everything has a lot to learn.

— 99 —

"

There is no job
so simple that
it cannot be
done wrong.

"

"

The trouble with mixing business and pleasure is that pleasure usually comes out on top.

"

———— **"** ————

Ideas are funny things. They don't work unless you do.

———— **"** ————

"

Choose a job you love, and you will never have to work a day in your life.

"

"

The person who marries for money usually earns every penny of it.

"

66

Our words
may hide our
thoughts, but
our actions will
reveal them.

99

"

It isn't what you know that counts, it's what you think of in time.

"

"

Be careful when you give advice — somebody might take it.

"

"

The older you get, the tougher it is to lose weight, because your body and your fat are friends.

"

“

There's nothing sweeter than the patter of little feet . . .going off to school.

”

——————— **"** ———————

If your motive is profit, then you may go broke. But if your motive is service, you will probably make a profit.

——————— **"** ———————

―――――――― 66 ――――――――

Everybody
makes a very
bad mistake
at least once
a week.

―――――――― 99 ――――――――

———— **66** ————

Even if you're on
the right track,
you'll get run
over if you just
sit there.

———— **99** ————

"

If men acted after marriage as they do during courtship, there would be fewer divorces — and more bankruptcies.

"

"

There are three ways to get something done: do it yourself, hire someone to do it, or forbid your kids to do it.

"

"

Adolescence
is the age when
children try to
bring up their
parents.

,,

66

Real men do eat quiche if they like it.

99

"

One trouble
with trouble is
that it usually
starts out
like fun.

"

—— **66** ——

When your head swells up, your brain stops working.

—— **99** ——

66

Behind every successful man stands a surprised mother-in-law.

99

"

Life not only
begins at forty
— it begins to
show.

"

"

The person
rowing the boat
seldom has time
to rock it.

"

—————— " ——————

There are three
kinds of friends:
best friends,
guest friends,
and pest friends.

—————— " ——————

—— **"** ——

Marriages are made in heaven — so are thunder and lightning.

—— **"** ——

———— " ————

You don't
have to brush
all of your teeth —
only the ones you
want to keep.

———— " ————

"

People who know the least always argue the most.

"

God is a
woman.

—— 66 ——

Santa Claus used to work for Federal Express.

—— 99 ——

"

You never have to explain something you haven't said.

"

66

Marriage is like twirling a baton, turning handsprings, or eating with chopsticks. It looks easy till you try it.

99

> **"**
> ─────────

It is especially
hard to work for
money you've
already spent for
something you
didn't need.

> ─────────
> **"**

---- **66** ----

Experts
don't know
either.

---- **99** ----

"

I cannot give you a formula for success, but I can give you the formula for failure: try to please everybody.

"

"

Even mothers
of hippos think
their children
are beautiful.

"

—— **66** ——

Opera in English is still opera.

—— **99** ——

—— **66** ——

One of the hardest decisions in life is when to start middle age.

—— **99** ——

——— 66 ———

Murphy's Law:

If anything can go wrong it will.

——— 99 ———

———— **"** ————

O'Toole's commentary on Murphy's Law: Murphy was an optimist.

———— **"** ————

"

The best way
to appreciate
your job is to
imagine yourself
without one.

"

" Marriage is compromise. "

"

Foolishness
always results
when the tongue
outraces the
brain.

"

——————— " ———————

The Golden Rule:

He who has
the gold makes
the rules.

——————— " ———————

Rule of Success:

Trust only those who stand to lose as much as you when things go wrong.

"

All children
are born with a
hearing problem.
They can hear
everyone but
their mother.

"

——————— 66 ———————

Few people
travel the road
to success
without a
puncture or two.

——————— 99 ———————

"

Hard work is the yeast that raises the dough.

"

"

To err is
human, to
forgive is not
company
policy.

"

66

Age doesn't
always bring
wisdom.
Sometimes age
comes alone.

99

"

Say no, then negotiate.

"

"

Everybody talks about the weather, but nobody seems to do much about it.

"

‟

Before you have an argument with your boss, take a good look at both sides — his side and the outside.

″

—— **66** ——

'Average but
works hard,'
beats 'brilliant
but lazy.'

—— **99** ——

"

Your grandma
was a libber,
too. She just
wasn't allowed
to say so.

"

"

All doctors should have at least one operation.

"

—————— " ——————

Be yourself.
Who else
is better
qualified?

—————— " ——————

66

The closest to
perfection a
person ever
comes is when
they fill out a job
application form.

99

"

When it comes to broken marriages, most husbands will split the blame — half his wife's fault, and half her mother's.

"

66

After all is said and done, more is said than done.

99

Other Great Quotations Books:

- Happle Birthday
- Best of Success
- Great Quotes/
  Great Leaders
- Aged to Perfection
- Retirement
- Love on Your
  Wedding...
- Cat Tales
- Thinking of You
- Words of Love
- Words for Friendship
- To My Love
- Inspirations
- Sports Quotes

- Never Never Quit
- Motivational Quotes
- Customer Care
- Commitment to
  Quaity
- Over the Hill
- Golf Humor
- Happy Birthday
  to the Golfer
- Handle Stress
- Great Quotes/
  Great Women
- A smiles increases
  your face Value
- Keys to Happiness
- Things you'll learn...

GREAT QUOTATIONS, INC.
919 SPRINGER DRIVE • LOMBARD, IL 60148 - 6416

TOLL FREE: 800-621-1432 (Outside Illinois)
(708) 953-1222